J E   Agle
         Three boys and a
tugboat.

187548

THREE BOYS
AND A TUGBOAT

by NAN HAYDEN AGLE and ELLEN WILSON

THREE · BOYS

AND A TUGBOAT

Illustrated by MARIAN HONIGMAN

CHARLES SCRIBNER'S SONS · New York

To RUTH and KITTY

and to ELEANOR

and JEAN

WITH GRATEFUL ACKNOWLEDGMENT

for help given by the Captain and crew of
the *Justine* of the Curtis Bay Towing
Company of Baltimore, Maryland, and
the Providence Steamboat Company of
Rhode Island.

CONTENTS

Chapter One

UNCLE STITCH

Right in the middle of the night there was a loud bang, bang on the front door.

The dog, John Paul Jones, rushed out from under the great big bed, barking furiously. Then he dashed down the stairs. What a racket! No one could stay asleep.

The three boys, Abercrombie, Benjamin and Christopher, sat up straight in the great big bed. Abercrombie was on the right-hand side. Benjamin was on the left-hand side and Christopher was in the middle.

"What's all the noise?" asked Abercrombie.

"What's John Paul Jones after?" asked Benjamin.

"Who's banging on the door?" asked Christopher.

And the three brothers jumped out of bed and ran down the stairs.

Abercrombie said, "Maybe it's a burglar."

Benjamin said, "Too much noise—maybe it's a fireman."

Christopher said, "No smoke—maybe it's a policeman."

At the foot of the stairs they bumped into their grandmother as she hurried toward the door in her plum-colored robe and slippers.

"Quiet, John Paul Jones, quiet," Gran said to the dog. Then she opened the door and in came a man.

He was not a burglar.

He was not a fireman.

He was not a policeman.

Instead, he was Uncle Stitch.

There was hugging and laughing and everybody talked at once and Gran said, "I might have known it was Stitch. Who else would pay a call at this late hour?"

Stitch was Father's youngest brother, Gran's youngest son, and the three boys' favorite uncle. Father was a lighthouse keeper but Uncle Stitch was captain of a tugboat.

Uncle Stitch was strong and dark. His voice was deep and loud. He smelled of a fresh breeze and he really knew how to tell a story.

The boys loved to hear Uncle Stitch talk about his adventures on his tug, the *Kittiwake*. But this night he had no time for stories. He had something more important to tell them.

"Get ready, boys," he said, "I'm taking you along with me. You are going to visit the *Kitti-wake*. Hurry, now. We've no time to lose. We must be aboard the tugboat by morning."

The three boys were so excited they nearly burst, for they had always wanted to visit the *Kittiwake*. They leaped about Uncle Stitch like hunting hound pups. They whacked him with their fists and shouted,

"Hurrah!"
"Yippee!"
"Hot dog!"

And John Paul Jones raced around in circles after his tail and barked his loudest bark. Uncle Stitch laughed but Gran did not laugh.

Gran put her hands over her ears to keep out the racket and said, "Not quite so fast, Stitch. Settle down for a while. Spend the night with us and we will talk about the trip in the morning. Come, I'll make you a cup of coffee."

"Can't wait a minute," Stitch told her. "We are shoving off right away. This is the first time I've been able to drive home for the boys. As you know, I've always wanted them to visit me. They have visited a lighthouse but I want them to feel a deck under their feet. I should have written ahead to ask them but what difference does that make to boys?" He turned to the boys and added, "Don't just stand there. Get a move on."

"You mean we are going right away?" asked Abercrombie.

"You mean we are going in the middle of the night?" asked Benjamin.

"You mean we are going without Gran?" asked Christopher.

"Yep," Captain Stitch said, nodding vigorously. "Right now, in the middle of the night, without Gran. That is if Gran says you may go."

The three boys turned from their uncle and threw themselves upon Gran. "May we go, Gran, please? Say we may, Gran."

And Abercrombie said, "We are quite grown up now, Gran."

And Benjamin said, "We will write to you, Gran."

And Christopher said, "We will mind Uncle Stitch and do everything he tells us to, Gran."

Gran was quiet. She wished that the boys could wait until morning. She wished that they had time to eat a big breakfast. She wished that she had time to press their Sunday suits.

However, after a while Gran said, "All right, boys, you may go with Uncle Stitch. Run along now. I'll make sandwiches while you dress. Be sure to take warm sweaters and your raincoats."

The boys shouted, "Thank you, Gran," and flew up the stairs, two steps at a time. John Paul Jones went barking after them.

"What fun to leave home in the middle of the night!" said Abercrombie as he packed his bag.

"What fun to ride in the jeep with Uncle Stitch!" said Benjamin as he packed his bag.

"What fun to visit the *Kittiwake*!" said Christopher as he packed his bag.

In no time the three boys thundered down the stairs again, two steps at a time. John Paul Jones followed close behind.

"We're ready to go, Uncle Stitch," they called out together. They stood in a row by the front door.

Dressed in dungarees and bright red sweaters, with raincoats over their arms, the three boys looked exactly alike. And no wonder!

Abercrombie, Benjamin and Christopher were triplets.

They looked alike, they talked alike, they worked and played and walked alike. They were so much alike in every way that no one could tell them apart, except Gran. Somehow Gran always knew which boy was which. Especially since they'd begun to part their hair!

Abercrombie parted his hair on the right.

Benjamin parted his hair on the left.

Christopher parted his hair in the middle and it wouldn't stay parted at all.

But tonight all three had forgotten to part their hair.

Uncle Stitch took one look at them and he roared with laughter.

"Wait till the crew of the *Kittiwake* sees you, boys. You look as much alike as three marlinspikes."

The boys laughed too, for they thought it was fun to look alike.

And Abercrombie said, "Yes, I look like Benjamin and Christopher but *I* want to be an explorer and discover new lands."

And Benjamin said, "I look like Christopher and Abercrombie but *I* want to be a zoo-keeper in charge of strange animals from all over the world."

And Christopher said, "I look like Abercrombie and Benjamin but *I* want to be an engineer and drive a fast train from one end of the country to the other."

Uncle Stitch said, "Well, no matter what you want to be, you will all three be sailors on the *Kittiwake.*"

At that, the boys grinned from ear to ear and all three grins were exactly alike.

Gran gave the boys a basket of fruit, a bag

of sandwiches and a hug apiece. And last of all she gave them some sound advice about clean teeth, plenty of sleep and manners while visiting.

The three boys told her good-by, then they ran out the door with John Paul Jones barking at their heels.

"Send that dog back," ordered Uncle Stitch. "You can't take him along. He'd be a nuisance on a tug, even if his name is John Paul Jones."

Hearing his name, the dog stopped and raised one ear. The boys stopped too.

Abercrombie frowned at Benjamin.

Benjamin frowned at Christopher.

Christopher frowned at Abercrombie.

Then they all began to talk at once. "He won't be any trouble. He's a member of the family. He always goes wherever we go. We never leave him home."

Uncle Stitch could see that he was out-numbered. He shook his head. "All right, all right. Have it your way. But you'll be sorry. Bring the dog but you'll have to keep your eye on him and keep him out of my way."

The boys shouted for joy. They piled into the back seat of Uncle Stitch's jeep. John Paul Jones lay on the floor.

Uncle Stitch took the driver's seat and off they went with a roar, the boys shouting, "Good-by, Gran, good-by."

John Paul Jones curled up at once on the floor of the jeep and went right to sleep, but the boys were wide awake. They sat on the edge of the seat, leaning forward. They were excited.

For some time they rode in silence, each boy thinking about tomorrow. What would it be like on a tugboat? Would the sea be rough the way it was around Father's lighthouse?

As the jeep bumped over the railroad track on the outskirts of town Benjamin asked,

"How big is the *Kittiwake*, Uncle Stitch?"

And Uncle Stitch told him, "She's bigger than she looks, Abercrombie."

Whereupon the other two boys said together, "He's not Abercrombie, he's Benjamin."

Uncle Stitch did not reply.

After a while Abercrombie asked,

"How fast can a tugboat go, Uncle Stitch?"

"Speed doesn't matter on a tug," Uncle Stitch told him. "It's power that is important and the *Kittiwake* is mighty powerful, Christopher."

Whereupon the other two boys said together, "He's not Christopher, he's Abercrombie."

Uncle Stitch did not reply. Instead, he pulled over to the side of the road and stopped the jeep. He turned around and flashed his flashlight on his three nephews. He examined the first boy, then the second, then the third. The three boys looked exactly the same.

Uncle Stitch stepped on the starter again and said, "I give up. You three look as much alike as three grommets. And you all three ask too many questions."

Abercrombie nudged Benjamin.

Benjamin nudged Christopher.

Christopher reached across Benjamin and nudged Abercrombie. Then they all grinned in the dark. It was fun being as much alike as three grommets, whatever they were.

They rode on for a mile or two without asking a single question, but finally Abercrombie said, "Uncle Stitch, what does the word *Kittiwake* mean?" And Uncle Stitch said, "A *Kittiwake* is a sea bird. It's small, chunky and a good swimmer. All of our tugboats are named for water birds: the *Puffin*, the *Plover*, the *Gannet*, and the *Auk*."

"Tell us all you know about tugboats, Uncle Stitch," the boys said next.

Uncle Stitch had to laugh. "It took me twenty-five years of hard work to learn all I know about tugs. Now you want me to tell you everything in one sentence. You do your own finding out yourselves while you are on the *Kittiwake*. And if you don't get some sleep tonight, you will be too tired to learn anything tomorrow."

Abercrombie, Benjamin and Christopher were sure that they were too excited to go to sleep. They were sure that the noisy, bumpy jeep would keep them awake. But they closed their eyes, and in no time they were all sound asleep.

They slept all night long. So did John Paul Jones.

Chapter Two

SEAPORT

The next thing the boys knew Uncle Stitch was calling them. "Wake up, you lazy landlubbers, wake up!"

"Where are we?" asked Abercrombie, parting his hair on the right.

"What time is it?" asked Benjamin, parting his hair on the left.

"Where is the tugboat," asked Christopher, not parting his hair at all.

Uncle Stitch looked at them and laughed.

"Now I know which boy is which," he said. "We are in Seaport, Abercrombie. We're on

18

the bluff where I live. It is nearly six o'clock on a fine morning, Benjamin. The tugs are below in the harbor, Christopher." And he asked, "Did I guess the right boy?" and the three boys nodded.

Stiffly they climbed out of the jeep. They yawned and stretched. It felt good to be up.

John Paul Jones yawned and stretched too. Then he sniffed the air and wagged his tail. Something must have smelled very fine, for he jumped to the ground and ran down the hill as fast as he could go.

The boys did not notice him at all. They were too much interested in Seaport.

"I smell the sea," said Abercrombie.

"It smells the way it does at the lighthouse," said Benjamin.

"Yes—it smells salty," said Christopher.

Uncle Stitch was pleased. He loved the sea

19

and everything about it. He wanted the boys to love it too. He hoped that someday they would follow the sea.

Uncle Stitch pointed and said, "There is Seaport harbor, boys; one of the busiest, most

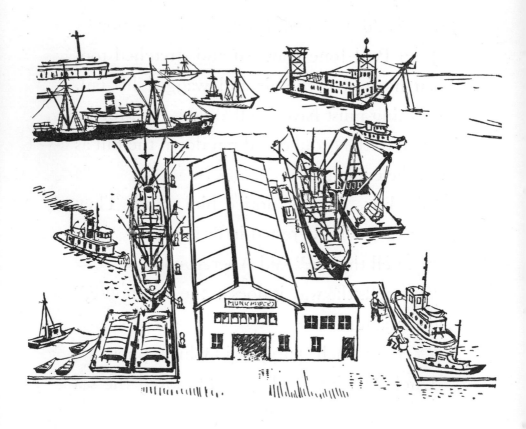

important ports in the country. Look at her, boys, look below."

The boys looked below.

At the foot of the bluff there were narrow streets. At the end of the streets lay the wharf.

Out beyond the wharf lay the harbor. And out from the harbor stretched the sea. It sparkled blue, then green, then blue again; never still, never the same.

Dotted here and there on the water were the boats and ships. There were little rowboats, middle sized motorboats and big ships. Some were tied at the piers. Others were anchored in the bay. The boys had never seen so many.

"Where are the tugs, Uncle Stitch?" asked Abercrombie.

"Which boat is yours, Uncle Stitch?" asked Benjamin.

"Which boat is the *Kittiwake*, Uncle Stitch?" asked Christopher.

"There comes a tug now, boys," Uncle Stitch told them briskly. "There beyond that oil tanker. Here she comes. Why, it's the *Kittiwake* herself! See her, boys? She's coming in from her night run. Look at her." And Uncle Stitch pointed proudly to a chunky brown boat that was chugging toward the shore.

Abercrombie looked at the tug. He was disappointed. "It's such a little boat," he said. He wished that Uncle Stitch were the captain of the big ocean liner anchored in the bay.

Benjamin looked at the tug. He was disappointed, too. "It's kind of ugly," he said. He wished that Uncle Stitch were the captain of the white freighter with the red trimmings.

Christopher looked at the tug. He was disappointed, too. "It's such a stumpy boat," he said. He wished that Uncle Stitch were the captain of the slim yacht with the tall mast.

Uncle Stitch frowned at Abercrombie. Then he said, "The *Kittiwake* is bigger than she looks."

He frowned at Benjamin. "She's as pretty as

23

a tug should be—and that's pretty enough for me."

He frowned at Christopher. "She's built for power, not for grace—and she's as strong as a whale."

Then to all three boys he said, "Every ship that comes into port or leaves port depends upon a tug to dock her and to help her out to the channel. If there were no tugboats, harbor traffic would be at a standstill."

"Really?"

"Truly?"

"Honestly?" asked the three boys. They were impressed.

Uncle Stitch said proudly, "Yes, tugboats are most important boats, and the *Kittiwake* is the best tug of them all." He thought awhile then added, "Let's go aboard her right now, boys. Grab your dunnage and follow me."

Uncle Stitch started down the hill, muttering to himself, "Little, ugly, stumpy! My *Kittiwake*. Wait till the boys know her. They'll sing another tune then."

The boys picked up their dunnage and followed him. Halfway down the hill Uncle Stitch stopped, turned around and asked, "Where is the dog?"

The boys stopped, too. Where was John Paul Jones?

Abercrombie looked at Benjamin.

Benjamin looked at Christopher.

Christopher looked at Abercrombie.

The three boys had been so busy thinking about boats, that not one of them had thought about the dog. Not one of them knew where he was.

They began to call, "Here, John Paul Jones! Here, John Paul Jones!"

They ran back up the hill, whistling and calling as they ran. "Here, John Paul Jones!"

John Paul Jones was nowhere in sight.

The boys ran every which way, calling and whistling. But they could not find him.

"Perhaps he is chasing a cat," suggested Abercrombie.

"Perhaps he is after a squirrel," suggested Benjamin.

"Perhaps he is with another dog," suggested Christopher.

Again the boys looked at one another. Their faces were solemn.

Abercrombie said, "Maybe he has been stolen."

Benjamin said, "Maybe he has been run over."

Christopher said, "Maybe the dog catcher caught him."

They ran down the hill again to Uncle Stitch. Uncle Stitch was cross over the delay.

"John Paul Jones is lost."

"What shall we do?"

"We can't go on the tug without him."

Uncle Stitch scolded them in a loud voice. "I told you to leave that dog home. I told you he'd be a nuisance. I told you to keep an eye on him. It's time to go aboard the *Kittiwake* now—dog or no dog."

The boys stood in a row and frowned at Uncle Stitch.

Uncle Stitch frowned back.

He said, "The dog will turn up later on. The men at the pier will watch out for him. Forget him and come along."

Abercrombie, Benjamin and Christopher looked at their uncle. Forget John Paul Jones? The idea! Why, he was one of the family.

Once more the boys called and called at the top of their voices. But John Paul Jones was nowhere in sight.

Uncle Stitch walked on impatiently.

The boys followed him slowly, without a word.

Uncle Stitch turned down a narrow street between high buildings. Suddenly the street ended. The buildings ended, too. There, straight ahead, lay the pier. And moored alongside the pier were five tugboats: the *Puffin*, the *Plover*, the *Gannet*, the *Auk*, and the *Kittiwake*.

Uncle Stitch stopped frowning as he hurried toward the *Kittiwake*. In three big strides he was over the side and on her deck.

The boys did not stop frowning. They did not follow him aboard. Instead, they stopped at the edge of the pier. They stood in a row, their faces solemn.

Abercrombie took a deep breath. "Please, Uncle Stitch, give us a few more minutes. I want to run down the wharf on that side." He pointed toward the right. "I'm pretty sure John Paul Jones is down there."

Benjamin said, "Please, Uncle Stitch. I want to run down the wharf on that side." He pointed toward the left. "I'm pretty sure John Paul Jones is down there."

Christopher said, "Please, Uncle Stitch. I want to run up the hill again." He waved his hand. "I'm pretty sure he's up there."

Uncle Stitch looked at his nephews doubtfully. "Very well, but be quick about it." Then he turned and went into the deckhouse.

Abercrombie flung his dunnage on the deck and ran down the wharf to the right. He passed a line of stevedores who were carrying great bunches of bananas on their shoulders.

"Have you seen a white dog with black spots?" Abercrombie asked them. The men shook their heads and went on.

Abercrombie hurried on to the corner. He stopped at a store filled with ropes, pulleys, fishing rods and crab nets.

"Have you seen a white dog with black spots?" he asked the storekeeper.

The storekeeper had not. So Abercrombie ran on until he met two sailors walking along. They had not seen the dog either. Abercrombie ran all the way to the end of the street. Not a single person had seen a white dog with black spots.

Benjamin flung his dunnage on the deck and ran down the wharf to the left. He stopped at a shed where men were sorting oysters into a barrel.

"Have you seen a dog about so high?" asked Benjamin.

One man pointed to a brown Chesapeake Retriever sleeping by the door. But Benjamin declared that he was too big and too brown.

He hurried on. He stopped at the corner where big nets were spread out to dry.

"Have you seen a dog, about so high?" he asked an old man who was mending a net.

The old man must have been deaf, for he didn't even look up from his work.

Benjamin stopped a man with a pushcart of vegetables, a woman sweeping her steps and the policeman. But not one of them had seen a dog—about so high.

Christopher flung his dunnage aboard the *Kittiwake* and ran past the *Puffin*, the *Plover*, the *Gannet*, and the *Auk*. He ran up the narrow street between high buildings. He ran all the way to the top of the hill.

To everyone he met he said, "Have you seen a strange dog? He answers to the name of John Paul Jones."

A boy said he had heard a dog barking earlier in the day. It might have been John Paul Jones.

A man said a strange dog had made friends

with his dog. It might have been John Paul
Jones.

A little girl said some dog had chased her cat
up a tree. The cat was still there but the dog was
gone.

Christopher whistled and called. Finally he
gave up and hurried back to the wharf.

At the wharf he met his brothers. They, too,
had given up the search. Discouraged, the three
boys walked slowly toward the *Kittiwake*.

"What will we do without John Paul Jones?"
they asked each other.

Slowly they climbed over the rail of the
Kittiwake and on to the deck.

And there, who should dash out to meet
them—but John Paul Jones himself! The boys
shouted for joy.

"He wasn't lost after all," said Abercrombie.

"He found the tug all by himself," said Benjamin.

"He knew all the time where we were going," said Christopher.

All together, boys and dog, they made so much noise that Uncle Stitch came out on deck. With him was a tall, thin man. When things were quieter, Uncle Stitch said,

"This is Mr. Foxworthy, the mate. And, Mr. Foxworthy, these are the new deckhands, Abercrombie, Benjamin and Christopher."

The boys liked Mr. Foxworthy at once. After shaking hands with him, they began to look around. Now that they had found John Paul Jones, they wanted to explore the *Kittiwake*. They wanted to see everything at once.

But Uncle Stitch said, "Breakfast first. This way to the galley."

"Galley? What's a galley?" asked the boys, as they followed Uncle Stitch. They all tried to squeeze through the deckhouse door at once, with John Paul Jones under their feet.

Chapter Three

THE
KITTIWAKE

This is the galley," said Uncle Stitch as the boys followed him into a neat little room filled with a delicious smell of coffee and bacon.

"It's a kitchen," said Abercrombie, as he looked at the stove and the sink.

"It's a dining room," said Benjamin, as he looked at the table against the bulkhead.

"Let's eat," said Christopher.

"First, meet the cook," said Uncle Stitch.

37

"Cook, let me introduce our new deckhands, Abercrombie, Benjamin and Christopher."

Cook turned from the stove and glanced at the boys. "Which is which?" he asked.

"I am Abercrombie. My hair parts on the right."

"I am Benjamin. My hair parts on the left."

"I am Christopher. My hair won't stay parted at all," said the boys, one after the other, as they hopped up on the bench.

"What do you want for breakfast?" asked Cook.

The boys thought for a minute.

"Pancakes and syrup for me," said Abercrombie.

"Bacon and eggs for me," said Benjamin.

"Lots of cereal for me," said Christopher. "I'm hungry."

Uncle Stitch, behind his morning newspaper, said, "Coffee with my bacon and eggs."

Cook poured out pancake batter with one hand. With the other he broke eggs into a frying pan. He reached for milk glasses with one hand and for cereal with the other.

The boys watched him with admiration.

"Why are the glasses kept in those holders?" asked Abercrombie.

"Why are the plates in racks?" asked Benjamin.

"Why is there a rail around the table?" asked Christopher.

"Come a blow, everything that's not nailed down would be on the floor," said Cook, as he put their breakfast before them.

For a while the boys stopped asking questions. As they ate, they thought about being deckhands.

Abercrombie thought maybe he'd give up

discovering new lands, and do his exploring on the sea.

Benjamin thought maybe he'd give up zoo-keeping, and sail on expeditions to collect wild animals.

Christopher thought maybe he'd give up the idea of being an engineer on a train, and be one on a ship, instead.

Uncle Stitch looked up from his paper. "Here's some news you boys will be interested in. The Seaport Zoo has bought two new bears. They arrive today from South America on the ship *Fortuna*."

"What kind of bears?" asked all the boys.

"They're called spectacle bears. They are black, with a circle of white fur around each eye. That makes them look as though they are wearing glasses. They are quite rare. These two little fellows are less than a year old."

"Gee, I'd like to see them," said Abercrombie.

"They must look funny with specs," said Benjamin.

"Can't we go to the zoo to see them tomorrow?" asked Christopher.

Uncle Stitch said, "Maybe we won't have to wait until tomorrow. Maybe we'll see the *Fortuna* when she docks. Maybe we'll even go to meet her. One of the tugs will be called for the job."

"Hope it's the *Kittiwake*," said all the boys.

"More coffee, Captain?" asked Cook.

"No, thanks. We'd better go along now, if these boys are to get acquainted with the *Kittiwake* before we shove off."

The boys hopped off the bench, thanked Cook for their good breakfast, and followed Uncle Stitch.

"First we'll visit the engine room," he said, and headed below.

"Gee, this stairway is narrow," said the boys.

"We don't call it a stairway. We call it a companionway. Can you remember that?" said Uncle Stitch.

The boys nodded.

"Whew, it's hot down here," they said, as they reached the engine room.

The engineer came forward to meet them. His name was MacIntosh.

"Mr. Mac," said Uncle Stitch, "I want you to show our new deckhands around. I have some work to do." And he went back up the companionway.

"Glad to see you, boys," said Mr. Mac, as he wiped his hands on an old cloth. "Look around."

Abercrombie, Benjamin and Christopher

looked around the engine room. Everything was shiny. There was a huge engine. It was painted silver and had brass trimmings. There were pumps and pipes, cylinders, rods, and gauges.

Mr. Mac smiled proudly. "This is a one thousand horsepower engine. She's an oil-fired steam engine and she can't be beat. The *Plover* and the *Auk* have Diesel engines. But give me steam every time."

Then Mr. Mac noticed the three boys. "Well, well, triplets, by George. Can the captain tell you three apart?"

The boys nodded, and started to tell him about their hair. But just then one bell sounded. The indicator on the engine room telegraph moved to "Slow ahead."

Instantly, Mr. Mac pulled the engine throttle to "Slow ahead." The huge thousand horsepower engine started. The boys scrambled up the companionway.

On deck it was cooler. They found John Paul Jones there with two young men who were dressed in old blue pants, tennis shoes and nothing else. Their backs were brown and muscular. Their shoulders looked strong.

They did not notice the boys. Dan, the red headed one was forward, coiling a line. Pete, short and stocky, was coiling a line on the after deck.

The boys could feel the *Kittiwake* throbbing under their feet. They liked that. John Paul Jones could feel it, too. But he did not like it. The *Kittiwake* pulled away from the pier and headed out of the harbor.

"Hurrah, we're off!" said Abercrombie.

"We're heading out to sea," said Benjamin.

"We're on our way," said Christopher.

Dan and Pete looked up noticing the boys
for the first time.

"Fetch my eye glasses, Pete," Dan said with
a grin. "I'm seeing double."

Pete, grinning, too, said, "I'm seeing triple, myself."

Then they both laughed and said, "Hello, boys. Who are you?"

"We are Abercrombie, Benjamin and Christopher. We are the new deckhands. And this is our dog, John Paul Jones."

John Paul Jones heard his name, but he did not wag his tail. He hung his head and rolled his eyes at the boys.

"What's wrong with you, John Paul Jones?" the boys asked.

Pete said, "I'd say he is seasick."

And he was.

Poor dog. He really was seasick, right on the deck, right in front of everybody. Poor John Paul Jones! He was no sailor. The three boys stood in a row and shook their heads.

"Well, what are you waiting for, deckhands?" Dan asked sharply. "Get a mop and swab that deck."

"Yes, sir," the boys answered.

Abercrombie ran to the galley for a mop.

Benjamin raced round the deck until he found a bucket.

Christopher made a bed for the dog in a coil of rope.

While all this was going on, the *Kittiwake* was chugging across the harbor. Seagulls sailed overhead. The water rippled gently, changing from blue to green to purple.

The *Kittiwake* stopped at Steeltown pier to pick up her tow.

Captain Stitch called down from the wheelhouse. "Those two scows are ours, Dan and Pete. Throw a line aboard, and let's get started. They're loaded with slag for Long Bridge. It'll take us half a day to get there."

"Yes, sir," Dan and Pete called back.

Then Uncle Stitch shouted, "If those boys worry you too much, send them up to me."

Dan and Pete laughed. "We've put them to work, sir. They won't be any bother."

The boys were glad to hear this, for they wanted to be good deckhands. Their father had taught them to be orderly, dependable and resourceful. They ran up and down the deck, trying to help. They got underfoot and that was about all. John Paul Jones lay still in the coil of rope, feeling miserable.

Dan expertly looped the tug's after towline over the strong cleat on the forward end of the first scow. Then he signaled Captain Stitch that all was ready.

Captain Stitch signaled the engineer, and the *Kittiwake* pulled away. The heavy hawser stretched, and the tug towed the two scows out into the channel and headed down the bay. A wide wake opened behind the scows. It spread until it reached the shores on either side.

The deckhands sat down to rest on the after deck. Mr. Mac came up from the engine room and stood in the doorway to cool off. Here he could visit with the crew and still keep one ear on the engine room.

"What's the big rat's nest on the front of the tug?" asked Abercrombie as he took off his shirt and shoes.

"What are the sandbags hanging outside the rail?" asked Benjamin as he took off his shirt and shoes.

"What are the shiny stumps with red stars on top?" asked Christopher as he took off his shirt and shoes.

Dan and Pete were busy mending a heavy hawser but they looked up and laughed.

"The rat's nest is the puddin, or puddin apron. It's made of strong rope woven like a net. It is a bumper to protect the boat when she pushes," Dan told them.

"And the sandbags are fenders," Pete put in. "They are made of rope, too. The shiny stumps as you call them are bitts. We take several turns of hawser around a bitt when we tow."

The boys wondered whether they would ever learn all about tugboats.

"If you want to learn, start now," Pete told them. "Take those pieces of line and splice them."

"How?" asked the boys eagerly.

Dan and Pete laid aside their own work and showed the boys how to join the two pieces of rope. They showed the boys how to unlay the line and tuck the ends in between the strands.

The boys worked hard, each one hoping to

be the first to master the job. The sun shone hot on their backs, but the breeze was cool.

John Paul Jones sighed. He crawled out of his bed and went inside the deckhouse. He couldn't get comfortable anywhere.

The *Kittiwake* chugged along. She passed a big ship anchored in the bay. Could that be the *Fortuna*, the ship with the bears? The boys waved and the men aboard ship waved back. But the big ship was not the *Fortuna*.

The tug passed a dredge at work. The boys waved and the men on the dredge waved back. She passed three small fishing boats. "Any luck?" the boys called out. The fishermen shook their heads.

The *Kittiwake* met another big ship coming up the bay, dead ahead. Could that be the *Fortuna*?

"Toot!" the *Kittiwake* blew. The big ship

answered with a deep "Haawn!" She wasn't the *Fortuna*.

"Ships say hello, too," remarked the boys.

"Ships say more than hello," Dan told them. "That one toot from the *Kittiwake* means, 'I will keep to the right of the channel' and the

ship's one blast means, 'I, too, will keep to the right of the channel.' "

"Don't boats ever toot just for fun?" the boys asked.

"Nope," answered both Dan and Pete.

Then they both went back to work. Dan was splicing a hawser. Pete was mending a heavy ball covered with woven rope on the end of a line.

The boys leaned over Pete, watching him closely. "What is that thing?" they asked.

"This is called a monkey fist," said Pete. "It's the weight on the end of the heaving line."

The boys sighed. "We never will learn all about tugs."

"There's Old Fort, boys," Mr. Mac called from the engine room door.

The boys looked up. Ahead was a small island with a fort on it.

"She used to guard the harbor, way back in the old days."

Mr. Mac went on. "But she's deserted now. You can't land there without a permit."

"Why not?" asked the boys.

Before Mr. Mac had time to answer, Cook poked his head out of the galley door and said, "Lunch!" The boys forgot everything else and ran to the galley.

After lunch the *Kittiwake* left the two scows loaded with slag at Long Bridge. She picked up two empty scows and towed them back up the bay.

All afternoon the boys kept a sharp lookout for the *Fortuna*. They couldn't see her anywhere. Late in the afternoon the tug left the empty scows at Steeltown and headed for home.

The sky was clear. The sun was hot. The sea rippled gently. The boys grew sleepy. John Paul Jones was still inside, feeling miserable. It had been a long day for the boys and a longer day for the dog.

It was supper time when the *Kittiwake* finally docked at her own pier.

John Paul Jones came out on deck and sniffed. Land at last! How good it smelled to him!

Dan was just about to throw the line ashore, when a loud voice shouted through a megaphone. Everyone stopped to listen. It was the dispatcher, calling from the window of the shore office.

"All tugs proceed to the head of the bay at once, and stand by for further orders," he said.

"What's up?"

"What's the matter?"

"What's happened?" asked the three boys, one after another.

Quickly the boys ran into the deckhouse, up the companionway, and all the way up to the pilothouse to find out.

John Paul Jones did not follow them. He was overjoyed to sniff the land. He wagged his tail.

56

Then he ran swiftly to the rail and jumped for the dock.

The *Kittiwake* was not quite close enough to shore. Poor John Paul Jones! He fell "ker-splash" right into the water.

No one on the tug saw him fall in.

No one on the dock saw him fall in.

No one anywhere saw him fall in.

John Paul Jones could not reach the dock; he could not reach the boat. He swam round and round in circles. Finally he turned and swam out into the harbor. No one saw him go.

Chapter Four

THE *FORTUNA*

When Abercrombie, Benjamin and Christopher burst into the pilothouse to find out what was wrong, they found Uncle Stitch at the wheel.

"Why call all of the tugs?"

"Why must they all go to the same place?"

"Why must they go anywhere this time of day?" asked the boys, one after the other.

"No time for questions," said Uncle Stitch sharply. "Sit down. Keep your eyes and ears open, and your mouths shut."

"Yes, sir." the boys said.

They hopped on the chart table and sat in a row. Here they could see out over the harbor in all directions. At the same time they could keep an eye on all that was going on in the pilot-house.

Abercrombie punched Benjamin and pointed to the big wheel with spokes. Benjamin punched Christopher and pointed to the compass in front of the wheel. It was a curious looking gadget, shiny brass and like a clock. Christopher reached over and punched Abercrombie. He pointed to another dial, the engine room telegraph. On it speeds were indicated like numbers on a clock.

Again the boys wondered if they ever could learn all about tugboats. They leaned forward and watched as Uncle Stitch signaled the engine room. He set the controls at "Stop." The

Kittiwake lost way and finally stopped. He set the controls at "Full astern." Slowly the *Kittiwake* reversed, churning the water rosy white.

She turned left, blew one sharp "Toot." She pulled ahead and started toward the mouth of the bay, controls set at "Full speed ahead."

Uncle Stitch turned and picked up the ship-to-shore receiver. "*Kittiwake* to shore. *Kittiwake* to shore," he said.

He switched the dial and the boys heard, "Come in, *Kittiwake*. Adam speaking." Captain Adam was the shore dispatcher, the man who gave the orders to all the tugs. The boys listened.

They thought Uncle Stitch sounded like a detective when he said, "*Kittiwake* headed southwest; ready for further orders."

Again Captain Adam spoke. "All tugs come in. Calling all tugs."

He waited a moment; then went on. "Attention tugboats. The *Fortuna* from South America has run aground. She is on the sandbar at the mouth of the bay. There is a chance that we may pull her off at high tide. High tide at seven. *Kittiwake* take charge."

"The *Fortuna*!" said Abercrombie.

"The ship with the bears!" said Benjamin.

"The *Kittiwake* to the rescue!" said Christopher.

"I thought I told you boys to be still," said Uncle Stitch.

The boys were quiet for a while.

Then Benjamin said, "Look!" and pointed.

The boys saw the *Auk* and the *Plover* coming along astern. Then they spotted the *Puffin* dead ahead. Another tug was on her starboard bow. All the tugs were headed for the mouth of the bay at full speed. It was like a boat race only much more exciting. The boys punched each other.

The pink was fading from the sky and from the water. By the time the tugs reached the mouth of the bay it was nearly dark.

There lay the *Fortuna*, grounded on the sandbar. What a big ship she was! She towered above the *Kittiwake*. She looked all right, not listing a bit. The boys were disappointed. They thought an emergency should look like one.

"Nothing wrong with the *Fortuna* at all," the boys said.

Uncle Stitch turned round and faced them. "She's aground," he said. "That is serious. If we can't get her off bottom before she settles, it may take thousands of dollars to float her."

The boys were impressed.

Uncle Stitch turned back to the wheel. He pulled the whistle cord signal. "Toot, toot."

The *Fortuna* answered with a deep, loud "Waaa, Waaaa."

The boys were excited.

The boys hopped off the ladder and ran down the companionway to the main deck.

On deck the boys sat down astern out of the way. Here they watched. The ship's lights were on, red light on the port side, green light on the starboard side and white light fore and aft.

Ahead they could see the *Plover* making fast at the stern of the *Fortuna*. The other tugs were on her starboard side with tow lines already aboard.

Pete and Dan set the ladder against the side of the ship and Uncle Stitch ran up and over the rail as nimbly as a red squirrel. A few minutes later the boys saw him high on the bridge of the *Fortuna*. He was talking to the captain.

"What's Uncle Stitch doing up there, Pete?" asked Abercrombie.

"Why is Uncle Stitch pointing this way and that?" asked Benjamin.

"What is Uncle Stitch going to do, Dan?" asked Christopher.

"Captain Stitch has complete charge," Pete told them proudly. "He's sizing up the situation. He's deciding what will be the best way to move the *Fortuna*."

"Just everybody push hard, that's all," said Abercrombie.

Pete shook his head. "It's not that easy, young fellow. You got to test the wind and tide and current. Then you got to push just so and pull just so when the tide is just so. On top of that you'd best pray. It's high tide now, boys. Watch."

The boys ran over to the rail and leaned out so as not to miss a thing.

Uncle Stitch blew a shrill whistle once.

Mr. Foxworth on the *Kittiwake* replied, "Toot."

Uncle Stitch then blew, "Wheee-wheee" and the *Kittiwake* said, "Toot, toot."

The *Kittiwake* backed, then nosed in close to the *Fortuna* until her puddin was against the ship's side. The *Plover* reversed away until her tow line was taut.

Once more Uncle Stitch gave a shrill whistle and the *Kittiwake* replied with one toot. Then she pushed hard, pressing her puddin against the *Fortuna* with all of her one thousand horsepower. The *Plover* reversed with her seven hundred horsepower. The other tugs did as they were told.

The *Fortuna* did not budge. She was so big. The tugs were so small.

With another "toot, toot," the *Kittiwake* pushed again. The *Plover* reversed and the other tugs did as they were told.

The boys wished they could help. It was hard to do nothing.

"Come on, *Fortuna*!" they shouted together.

All at once a trembling shook the big ship.

"Hurrah!" yelled the boys. The men shouted, too.

The *Fortuna* shivered. Slowly she moved back into the channel.

The three boys ran up and down the deck, calling at the top of their voices. "Hurrah for the *Kittiwake*! Hurrah for Uncle Stitch!" They ran close to the rail and waved to the *Fortuna*.

A light from the big ship shone full on the

three boys. A sailor, looking down at them, shouted something in a strange language. Soon several other sailors gathered at the rail. They, too, looked down. They pointed at the boys; then laughed together.

"What are they laughing at?" the boys asked each other.

In a few moments Uncle Stitch's head appeared. He called down to them, "The men say they have never seen three boys who look exactly alike. They want you all to come aboard, so they can meet you."

The boys laughed. What fun to look alike! What fun to go aboard a big ship!

Together they called out, "Yes, yes! We will come aboard. May we see the bears?"

Uncle Stitch nodded "yes" and beckoned to them.

Once again, Pete placed the ladder against

the *Fortuna*, and said, "Up you go, boys, and watch your step."

The ladder was steep and narrow.

The *Fortuna* was big and tall.

The three boys were scared.

"You go first, Benjamin," said Abercrombie politely standing aside.

"Oh no, you go first, Christopher," said Benjamin politely standing aside.

"Oh no, you go first, Abercrombie," said Christopher politely standing aside.

Above, the men laughed heartily and Uncle Stitch shouted, "First man up is the best sailor!"

Such a scramble followed. The boys went up the ladder all at once and so fast that no one ever knew which boy was first to reach the top.

The sailors lifted the boys over the rail and stood them in a row on the deck of the *Fortuna*. The boys grinned at them.

The sailors chattered away in Spanish. They laughed and joked together as they examined the boys from tip to toe.

"Now may we see the bears?" asked the boys all together.

The mate who could speak English said, "Come with me."

He started aft. The boys and Uncle Stitch followed.

"Where do they keep animals on a ship?" asked Benjamin.

"Usually," said Uncle Stitch, "their cages are on the open deck. That's so the animals will get lots of fresh air. They can be fed and watered easily, too."

The mate of the *Fortuna* led Uncle Stitch and the boys in and out among the crates that were stacked on deck.

"Here we are," said the mate. He stopped before a large cage between two huge packing cases.

Abercrombie, Benjamin and Christopher poked each other with excitement. They crowded around the mate. But the mate stood stock still with his mouth open. Then he pointed to the cage.

The door of the cage was wide open.

The cage was empty.

Chapter Five

THE SEARCH

For a second, the boys did not realize what had happened. They looked into the empty cage. Then all together they asked, "Where are the bears?"

The mate did not answer. Turning, he ran to the captain of the *Fortuna*. He talked very fast in Spanish and waved his arms excitedly. The captain began to shout orders. Men ran back and forth, in and out. An alarm bell rang. It rang shrill and loud. The boys clapped their hands over their ears.

Uncle Stitch strode over to the *Fortuna*'s captain with the boys right behind him. After a few minutes of rapid talk with the captain, Uncle Stitch turned to Abercrombie, Benjamin and Christopher.

"Boys," Uncle Stitch said, "the bears have escaped. The sailors will search aboard ship and the captain wants our tug to search for them in the water. Come, let's get back to the *Kittiwake* at once."

Abercrombie, Benjamin and Christopher ran to the side of the ship and looked over the rail. Below they could see the *Kittiwake*, looking small. They could see Dan and Pete at the foot of the steep ladder. It made the boys dizzy to look down and see the black water around the *Kittiwake*.

Uncle Stitch hopped on the ladder and started down backwards, hand over hand.

Abercrombie hesitated. Then he said, "Me first," and hopped on the ladder. He started down, hand over hand.

Benjamin hesitated. Then he said, "Me second," and started down.

Christopher hesitated. Then he said, "Me last," and started down.

Down they went, hand over hand. The ladder was long, narrow and steep. They were glad when Dan and Pete grabbed hold of them and helped them to safety. It was good to feel the deck of the *Kittiwake* under their feet again.

Uncle Stitch was already telling the crew about the bears. Dan and Pete stood by the ladder, listening. Mr. Mac had poked his head out of the engine room to listen. Cook leaned out the companionway, and Mr. Foxworthy looked out the pilothouse window. All of them listened

carefully to Uncle Stitch. The three boys listened, too.

"The ship's captain offers two hundred dollars reward for the capture of the bears—one hundred for each," said Uncle Stitch. "The *Fortuna*'s crew is hunting in every corner of their ship, but they might have jumped overboard. The captain tells me that most bears cannot swim but these spectacle bears are fine swimmers. We will search the water nearby. Turn on the searchlight. Prepare to lower the lifeboat. Stand by with nets and ropes."

Uncle Stitch ran up to the pilothouse. Mr. Mac ran below to the engine room. Cook came out on deck to help. The boys ran to the rail to watch.

Everything happened at once. On went the searchlight. Out over the water swung the lifeboat. Out came the nets and ropes. "Toot, toot" signaled the whistle.

The *Kittiwake* pulled away from the *Fortuna* and started on the search.

"I hope we see the bears first," said Abercrombie.

"Me, too," said Benjamin. "But it's not going to be easy to see black bears in this black water."

"Don't forget those white rings around their eyes. Those specs ought to help us spot them," said Christopher.

The powerful light moved slowly back and forth, back and forth over the dark water. The boys looked and looked but there was no sign of the bears.

For over an hour the *Kittiwake* circled round and round in the bay finally cruising back toward the harbor. Uncle Stitch searched every inch of the water. He turned the powerful light along the piers and along the shipyards. Still there was no sign of the missing bears.

Abercrombie, Benjamin and Christopher had been looking so long and so hard that they could scarcely keep their eyes open.

"I'm tired," Abercrombie said finally.

"I'm hungry," said Benjamin.

"I'm sleepy," said Christopher.

"No wonder," said Uncle Stitch, who had come up beside them. "You have had a long, hard day. Get Cook to give you some supper, then go up and lie down on my bunk for a while."

"But what if you find the bears while we are eating?" asked Abercrombie.

"What if you find them while we are lying down?" asked Benjamin.

"Or what if you find them while we are asleep?" asked Christopher.

"If we find the bears, I'll call you—even if you're asleep. I promise. We'll stop the search at midnight, anyhow, and tie up at the pier. Get some rest now, boys."

The boys walked slowly into the galley. They ate the sandwiches and milk that Cook gave them.

As he took his last swallow of milk, Abercrombie said sleepily, "We haven't seen John Paul Jones for a long time."

Benjamin said, "No we haven't. Where *can* he be?"

Christopher said, "He's probably asleep somewhere. Maybe he's in the cabin."

But when the boys dragged their tired feet into the cabin, John Paul Jones was not there.

"I wish he were here with us," said Abercrombie. He yawned as he climbed onto the side of the bunk nearest the wall.

"Oh, he's around somewhere," said Benjamin. He yawned as he climbed into the middle of the bunk.

"He'll probably be right here on the floor beside us by morning," said Christopher. He yawned, too, and climbed onto what little was left of the bunk.

"Can't you move over a little, Abercrombie?" asked Benjamin. But there was no answer. Abercrombie was sound asleep.

"Can't you move over a little, Benjamin?" asked Christopher. But there was no answer. Benjamin was sound asleep.

"I'll never be able to sleep in this tiny space," thought Christopher. Then he, too, fell asleep.

Next morning Abercrombie rolled over and bumped into Benjamin.

Benjamin rolled over and bumped into Christopher.

Christopher rolled over and fell out of the bunk.

When he hit the floor, all three boys woke up and laughed. They could feel the *Kittiwake* getting under way for the day's work. They could see out the porthole that the tug was pulling away from the wharf.

Abercrombie said, "No dressing, we're all dressed."

Benjamin said, "No teeth brushing, we have no tooth brushes."

Christopher said, "No face washing, no one here to tell us we have to."

They laughed to think what Gran would say. Then thinking of her they did comb their hair.

Abercrombie parted his on the right.

Benjamin parted his on the left.

But Christopher's would not stay parted at all.

As they started out the door the boys stopped. "John Paul Jones is not here!" they said together.

They ran out on deck calling, "John Paul Jones, here John Paul Jones!" They ran up the companionway calling, "John Paul Jones!"

They ran into the pilothouse where they found Mr. Foxworthy at the controls. "Have you seen John Paul Jones?" the boys asked breathlessly.

"No—and there is no news of the bears either," he told them. The boys were unhappy. They stood silently for some time. Then Mr. Foxworthy went on, "When we tied up last night the crew went ashore to sleep—all but Captain Stitch. He slept aboard. Today we will keep a sharp lookout for the bears while we are at work."

"And we'll keep a sharp lookout for John Paul Jones."

It was a beautiful day, bright and windy. A small boat with a loud motor went roaring past. Along the bank some boys were flying a kite. Somewhere in the distance a dog barked.

The boys looked up.

"That's not John Paul Jones' bark," said Abercrombie.

"No, John Paul Jones barks deeper than that," said Benjamin.

"John Paul Jones barks louder than that," said Christopher.

The boys ran into the galley. Cook was there. Uncle Stitch was there, reading the paper. But John Paul Jones was not there.

"Good morning, boys," said Uncle Stitch.

"Have some breakfast—and listen to this."

The boys hopped up in their places while Uncle Stitch read to them from the morning paper. "Lost: two bears from the ship *Fortuna*. Two hundred dollars reward for their capture. The bears are about four feet high, weigh one hundred and fifty pounds each, black with white circles around eyes. They eat roots and berries, can swim and fish."

"Gee, I wish we could find them," said Abercrombie.

"Me, too. I'd give anything to see them," said Benjamin.

"Me, too. I'd like to win that two hundred dollars," said Christopher.

"What would you do with two hundred dollars?" asked Cook.

"I'd buy a rowboat," said Abercrombie.

"I'd buy a sailboat," said Benjamin.

"I'd buy a motorboat," said Christopher.

"Two hundred dollars would hardly do all that," laughed Uncle Stitch, "but it would be a start."

The boys ate their breakfast, thinking about capturing the bears and winning the reward.

It was fun to eat while the tug was under way. The milk shook itself into circles in the glasses. The cereal jiggled in the bowls. The boys took their last bites and ran out on deck.

"What shall we do first?" asked Abercrombie.

"Let's start looking for the bears," said Benjamin.

"No, first of all, let's find John Paul Jones," said Christopher.

The other two boys agreed.

Again they looked in the pilothouse. They looked in the engine room. They looked on deck. Still no John Paul Jones. Where was their dog?

They began to worry in earnest.

Dan and Pete said they hadn't seen the dog for a long time. "Maybe he's in a corner somewhere, seasick again," they said.

But John Paul Jones was not to be found— not anywhere.

Now the boys really were worried.

They whistled and called. But no dog barked an answer. No John Paul Jones came rushing to greet them.

They went to tell Uncle Stitch. They found him at the wheel in the pilothouse. But he wasn't at all helpful.

"I told you not to bring that dog in the first place," he said.

The boys nodded sadly again.

"I told you to look after him if you brought him."

Abercrombie didn't dare look at the others for fear tears would come.

Benjamin didn't dare look at the others for fear he would cry.

Christopher didn't dare look at anyone for fear he might cry, too.

Uncle Stitch turned back to the wheel. "You found him before when you thought he was lost. You'll find him again, no doubt. Get to work and forget him. I thought you were deck-hands."

"Yes, sir," the boys said.

All that morning they helped Dan and Pete. They learned to ease out the heavy mooring line like old deckhands.

They tried not to worry about John Paul

Jones, but they couldn't help it. They worried while the *Kittiwake* took a ship to dry dock. They worried while she hauled a tanker to Steeltown and back. They worried while she nudged a banana boat out into the channel.

Once when they passed Old Fort Island, Abercrombie said, "Listen. Do you hear something?"

"Only the wind," answered Benjamin and Christopher.

Later, when they passed Old Fort Island again, Benjamin said, "Listen. Do you hear barking or anything?"

"Just the seagulls," answered Abercrombie and Christopher.

Still later, when they passed the island once more, Christopher said, "Listen. I do hear something. And it does sound like barking. Can you see anything?"

The boys looked hard, but they couldn't see a thing.

"Quick, let's get the spyglasses," they said.

All three boys ran up the companionway to the boat deck. They ran up the next companionway to the pilothouse.

"Lend us your spyglasses quick, Uncle Stitch. We want to look at something on Old Fort Island."

But Uncle Stitch said that Mr. Foxworthy had the glasses. He was watching for the bears. When they found Mr. Foxworthy he said Mr. Mac had the glasses. He was looking for the bears. Mr. Mac said that Cook had borrowed the glasses. Cook said Dan and Pete had taken them. Everyone had been looking for the bears at some time or other during the morning.

But Dan and Pete said they had taken the glasses back to the pilothouse. Sure enough.

There they were, hanging in their proper place in the pilothouse, right under Uncle Stitch's nose.

It was too late for the boys to watch Old Fort through the spyglasses.

By now it was past four o'clock in the afternoon. The *Kittiwake*'s work was over for the day. She left Old Fort behind and headed for home.

"Probably it was the wind you heard," said Uncle Stitch.

"Or the seagulls," said Dan and Pete.

"Or John Paul Jones," said Abercrombie, Benjamin and Christopher.

Chapter Six

THE OLD FORT

The *Kittiwake* was tied at the pier for the night. The crew was ready to go ashore.

The boys stood in a row in front of Uncle Stitch and would not budge.

"Please help us," begged Abercrombie.

"Please take us out to Old Fort," said Benjamin.

"We have to find out if John Paul Jones is really there," said Christopher.

Uncle Stitch was annoyed. "I've told you that there is a law forbidding anyone to land there without a permit and besides, work is over for the day."

"But this is an emergency," said Abercrombie.

Benjamin and Christopher agreed and so did the crew of the *Kittiwake*.

Uncle Stitch looked sharply at his crew. "Well," he said slowly, "I see I'm outnumbered again. All right. I will try to get permission to land on Old Fort."

And with that he turned to the ship-to-shore phone and called Mr. Adam.

"Who owns Old Fort Island?" Uncle Stitch asked.

"Coast Guard, I think," said Mr. Adams.

So Uncle Stitch called the Coast Guard.

"Who owns Old Fort Island?" he asked.

"Navy Department, I think," a voice answered.

So Uncle Stitch called the Navy Department.

"Seaport Historical Society, I think," a voice answered.

So Uncle Stitch called the Seaport Historical Society.

"Colonial Dames, I think," a voice answered.

So Uncle Stitch called the Colonial Dames.

"Well, now, let me think," a woman's voice answered. "It might be the Coast Guard."

"No, we tried them," said Uncle Stitch.

"Or the Navy Department."

"No, we tried them," said Uncle Stitch.

"Or the Seaport Historical Society."

"No, we tried them," said Uncle Stitch. "They said to call you."

By now Uncle Stitch was cross.

"Well, now, let me think," said the woman's voice. "Why don't you try the Port Authority?"

"Of course," said Uncle Stitch. "Why didn't I think of that in the first place?"

So he called the Port Authority.

"The State owns Old Fort Island. Why?" answered a brisk voice.

"Because I want to get permission to land there," said Uncle Stitch. "Who can give it to me?"

"We can," said the brisk voice. "But only in an emergency."

"Well, this is an emergency," said Uncle Stitch.

And he explained all about the three boys and John Paul Jones.

Abercrombie punched Benjamin.

Benjamin punched Christopher.

Christopher punched Abercrombie.

There was a long pause—"All right," came the answer at last, "you may land on Old Fort."

And the boys heard the click of the receiver.

"Yippee," cried the boys, pounding each other on the back.

Uncle Stitch sighed loudly, "I knew from the beginning that we should never have brought that dog!"

"Don't you worry, Uncle Stitch, we will help you," they said.

Uncle Stitch turned back to the controls. He reached for the bell pull. "Ding, ding."

The *Kittiwake* backed away from the pier.

"Ding" and the *Kittiwake* stopped. She swung around with her bow headed toward the open harbor.

"Ding" and she was chugging away again.

Uncle Stitch signaled Mr. Mac down in the engine room for more power. The *Kittiwake* went full speed ahead.

"Good old *Kittiwake*," said the boys proudly.

"She's not so little," said Abercrombie. "She's bigger than she looks."

"She's not so ugly," said Benjamin. "She's as pretty as a tug should be."

"She's not so stumpy," said Christopher. "And she's as strong as a whale."

Uncle Stitch didn't speak but he smiled.

Once more the *Kittiwake* passed the black channel buoy. It was on the right. She passed the red channel buoy. It was on the left. She passed a ship anchored off shore. Now she headed for Old Fort Island.

Abercrombie reached for the spyglasses.

"See anything?" asked Benjamin and Christopher eagerly.

"Nothng but rocks," said Abercrombie.

He passed the glasses to Benjamin.

"See anything?" asked Abercrombie and Christopher.

"Nothing but waves on the rocks," said Benjamin.

He passed the glasses to Christopher.

"See anything?" asked Abercrombie and Benjamin.

"No," said Christopher. "Just seagulls swooping around."

Uncle Stitch signaled Mr. Mac in the engine room to slow down. He leaned out the pilot house and called to Dan and Pete below. "Prepare to lower the lifeboat. Stand by to make a landing."

Soon they were as close to the island as they dared go in the *Kittiwake*. "Ding," Uncle Stitch gave the signal to stop.

He gave orders. Mr. Foxworthy and Mr. Mac and Cook were to stay on the *Kittiwake*. Dan and Pete were to row to shore in the lifeboat with Uncle Stitch.

Uncle Stitch looked at the boys doubtfully.

"Us, too," begged the boys. "Please let us go ashore in the lifeboat?"

"We'll hold on tight," said Abercrombie.

"We'll sit very still," said Benjamin.

"We won't fall in. And even if we do, we're very good swimmers," said Christopher.

Uncle Stitch looked out over the water, thinking.

"All right," he said at last. "Come along." The lifeboat swung out over the side of the tug and settled on the water.

Uncle Stitch jumped in and sat in the bow.

Dan and Pete jumped in and sat by the oars.

One after another the boys jumped in and sat in the stern.

Dan and Pete bent over the oars and off they went to Old Fort.

Uncle Stitch kept a sharp eye out for rocks and gave directions.

Abercrombie, Benjamin and Christopher sat still and did not say a word.

When they were in shallow water, several feet from the little island, Uncle Stitch said, "All right, boys. Roll up your dungarees and let's go. Dan, you and Pete stay here with the boat while the boys and I go ashore."

The boys rolled up their pants and Uncle Stitch took off his shoes and rolled up his pants. The boys jiggled so much in their excitement that they nearly tipped over the lifeboat.

"Hey!" called out Dan. "A fine bunch of sailors you turned out to be."

Uncle Stitch laughed as he straddled the rail of the boat and slipped into the water. The water was waist high and cold for summertime.

Uncle Stitch steadied the boat while the three boys slid into the water one after the other.

"Whee, it's cold!" said Abercrombie.

"Golly, it's rocky on the bottom!" said Benjamin.

"Something bit my toe," said Christopher.

Uncle Stitch laughed again and the four of them waded ashore splashing each other as they hurried.

Two seagulls circled silently overhead as they scrambled ashore. There was not a sign of life anywhere. The old stone fort, big and gloomy, took up most of the little island.

The whole place was scary.

The boys stood close together by Uncle Stitch and said nothing. The water ran down their legs and made puddles at their feet.

"There's nothing here, boys," Uncle Stitch told them, "We might as well go back."

The boys were about to agree with him when they heard a loud familiar bark. Out of a hole in the crumbling foundation came John Paul Jones!

Such excitement! The boys shouted for joy. The dog barked and dashed round and round, leaped at the boys and nearly wagged himself in two. Uncle Stitch kept saying, "Well, well, well—the boys were right after all." But no one heard him.

Finally when the din quieted down Abercrombie asked, "How do you suppose John Paul Jones got here?"

Uncle Stitch answered, "He must have fallen off the tug somehow and tried to swim after us. The tide must have swept him along until he reached this island. Come on, let's get back to the boat."

And the boys said, all three together, "Good old John Paul Jones! He's some swimmer!"

Uncle Stitch nodded agreement—then he started back. But John Paul Jones did not follow. Instead, he ran off into the fort, barking and barking. He ran back, looked at the boys, then ran off again, still barking.

"We've got to explore the fort, Uncle Stitch. John Paul Jones wants us to look at something," the boys said.

Then the three boys ran after John Paul Jones. Up over rocks, in through a door in the thick gray wall of the fort. John Paul Jones ran on ahead, down a worn stone walk to another door in the wall. Here he stopped and barked sharply. The boys ran to him.

The heavy wooden door was part way open. The boys peered in beyond it.

"It's pitch black in there," said Abercrombie, drawing back.

"I see two eyes shining," said Benjamin.

"I see four eyes shining," said Christopher.

"You go in first and see what's there," said Christopher to Benjamin.

"No, you go in first," said Benjamin to Abercrombie.

Just then the eyes started coming toward them. The boys stepped back. As they watched, the eyes came closer. Suddenly a streak of sunlight fell through the door, showing white circles around the eyes.

"The spectacle bears!" cried the three boys all together. Then they yelled at the top of their voices, "Uncle Stitch, Uncle Stitch, come quick!"

Chapter Seven

THE REWARD

Uncle Stitch ran into the fort and down the worn brick path.

"Look—look—Uncle Stitch!" the boys shouted to him. Uncle Stitch, quite breathless, leaned over the boys' shoulders and looked through the half open doorway.

There were the spectacle bears standing just inside. They were round and black. White rings showed up clearly around their sad brown eyes. They stood close together and blinked in the bright sunlight.

At first the boys were frightened.

"Shut the door," said Abercrombie.

"Lock the bears in," said Benjamin.

"Don't let them get away," said Christopher.

Then the three boys threw themselves against the old door.

The door creaked but did not shut. The rusty hinge broke in two. The latch and bolt came off and fell to the ground.

"Oh, well," the boys said as they backed away, "they are such young bears they wouldn't hurt a fly."

At that, Uncle Stitch stepped up and said, "All bears are dangerous. No bear is safe for boys to handle. You three take your dog back to the *Kittiwake* at once. Tell Mr. Foxworthy to call the shore office and have them send the bears' cage from the *Fortuna*. One of the tugs can pick it up for us. Hurry, I will stay here and guard the door."

The boys were disappointed.

"We don't want to go back now. We want to stay with the bears," said Abercrombic.

"We found the bears and we want to guard them," said Benjamin.

"You go back, Uncle Stitch. There are three of us," said Christopher.

Uncle Stitch cleared his throat loudly and frowned. "You heard the captain's orders. Obey them at once," he said sternly.

"Yes, sir!"

Just then, one of the bears went "woof" and dug at the door-sill with long white claws.

Such a scramble! The boys fell over each other getting out of the way. Christopher snatched up John Paul Jones right in the middle of a bark, and off they ran; out of the fort, down the slope. Without slowing up they splashed out into the water to the lifeboat.

As soon as Dan and Pete heard Captain Stitch's orders they picked up the oars and rowed fast.

In no time they were all aboard the *Kittiwake*.

As soon as Mr. Foxworthy heard Captain Stitch's orders he called the shore office. Captain Adam told him that he would send the *Plover* with the cage at once.

Everybody sat down to wait. They waited and they waited.

The boys were impatient. When would that tug come? They got up, they sat down, they walked up and down the deck wondering what the bears were doing.

At last Mr. Mac called out, "Here she comes!"

The boys ran to the rail and, sure enough, there was the *Plover*. She was coming at full speed with a lacy white spray at her bow—"a bone in her teeth" Mr. Mac called it.

The boys were excited.

The *Plover* pulled along side and lowered the big cage into the lifeboat. Dan and Pete had a hard time to keep it plumb.

The three boys begged to go to the fort with the cage. Mr. Foxworthy said, "No, you boys stay here." And he was in command while the captain was not on board.

The lifeboat pulled for the fort.

The *Plover* returned to port.

The boys waited again.

They sat down on the forward deck. Mr. Foxworthy and Mr. Mac and the cook sat with them. So did John Paul Jones.

They waited and waited and waited.

"Maybe the bears got away," suggested Abercrombie.

"Maybe Uncle Stitch can't get 'em into the cage," suggested Benjamin.

"Maybe the bears ate Uncle Stitch," suggested Christopher.

Mr. Foxworthy and Mr. Mac laughed and they both agreed that it would take a pretty clever bear to outsmart a tugboat captain.

"Here they come," the cook said.

The boys jumped to their feet and nearly fell overboard as they watched the lifeboat. Dan and Pete were pulling hard and Uncle Stitch was standing amidship balancing the big cage.

"They've got 'em! They've got the bears!" yelled the boys as the lifeboat pulled alongside. John Paul Jones raced up and down the deck barking like mad.

It was not easy to hoist the cage aboard the

Kittiwake but the crew managed after a struggle. As soon as the cage hit the deck, everybody gathered around to see the bears.

The cubs were charming. They sat close together in the middle of the cage looking wide

eyed and innocent. It made everyone laugh to see them peering through their round white spectacles. The boys wished they would "woof" again now that they were safely behind bars but the bears were too scared for that.

Uncle Stitch went up to the pilothouse and signaled the engine room, "Full speed ahead." Once more the deck of the *Kittiwake* shook under the boys' feet.

John Paul Jones felt the motion too, but he did not droop. In fact he wagged his tail.

"Why, John Paul Jones isn't seasick any more!" said Abercrombie.

"John Paul Jones likes being a sailor at last," said Benjamin.

"Yes, John Paul Jones is a sea-dog now," said Christopher.

"He is so glad to be back with his family

again," said Mr. Foxworthy, "he's forgotten that he ever was a poor sailor."

What fun! The three boys whooped for joy.

And everybody was happy when the *Kittiwake* docked at her pier.

Captain Stitch and his crew were proud of a job well done.

The Captain of the *Fortuna* came aboard. He was pleased to have the bears safe. He handed the reward to Uncle Stitch at once—two hundred brand new one dollar bills in a blue envelope.

But Uncle Stitch said *he* couldn't keep the reward. The three boys had really found the bears.

And the boys said, "We didn't find the bears. John Paul Jones was the one who really found the bears. John Paul Jones was the hero!"

Everybody agreed that John Paul Jones was the hero. But Uncle Stitch said, "What would a dog do with two hundred dollars? He has three boys of his own and plenty to eat. That's all he wants."

So it was decided that the reward should go to the three boys.

Uncle Stitch handed over the blue envelope. "You be the treasurer and take care of this two hundred dollars, Abercrombie," he said.

"I'll be treasurer. But I'm not Abercrombie. I am Benjamin."

Uncle Stitch looked at him. "But your hair is parted on the right," he said.

The boys looked at each other. Something had happened! The salty sea air had played tricks with their hair.

Now Abercrombie's hair was parted on the left.

Now Benjamin's hair was parted on the right.

And Christopher's hair was parted in the middle.

The boys grinned. Their grins were exactly alike.

Uncle Stitch said, "This is most confusing." The crew of the *Kittiwake* agreed.

But John Paul Jones was not confused. He just didn't care which boy was which.

"What are you going to do with all that money?" Uncle Stitch asked the three boys.

"We will give it to Gran to keep for us," said Abercrombie.

"We'll add to it and add to it," said Benjamin.

"And some day we'll have enough to buy a tugboat of our own," said Christopher.

Then the three boys said together, "A tugboat just like the *Kittiwake*."

Uncle Stitch smiled.

John Paul Jones wagged his tail.